This LADYBIRD TALE
belongs to

....

Little Red Riding Hood

Retold by Vera Southgate M.A., B.COM
with illustrations by Marina Le Ray

LADYBIRD TALES

ONCE UPON A TIME there was a little girl who was loved by everyone who knew her.

Her grandmother was so fond of her that she delighted in giving her presents. She made her a beautiful cape and hood of red velvet.

The little girl liked it so much that she never went out without wearing it. In time, everyone called her "Little Red Riding Hood".

Little Red Riding Hood lived with her mother and father in a small cottage near the edge of a large forest.

Her father was a woodcutter and worked all day in the forest.

Little Red Riding Hood loved her grandmother just as much as her grandmother loved her. Nearly every day she went along the path, through the forest, to visit her.

One day, Little Red Riding Hood's mother said, "Little Red Riding Hood, I have put a cake and a bottle of blackcurrant juice in this basket. I want you to take them to your grandmother. She is ill and they will do her good."

"Keep to the path and do not wander off into the forest," warned Little Red Riding Hood's mother.

"Don't worry, I shall take care," promised Little Red Riding Hood, as she took the basket and waved goodbye to her mother.

Before she had gone very far along the path through the forest, Little Red Riding Hood met a wolf.

She had never seen a wolf before and she did not know what a wicked creature he was. She thought he was a large dog and she was not in the least afraid of him.

"Good morning, Little Red Riding Hood," said the wolf.

"Good morning, sir," she replied.

"Where are you going to so early in the morning?" asked the wolf.

"To my grandmother's," Little Red Riding Hood replied.

"And what have you got in your basket?" the wolf went on.

"A cake and a bottle of blackcurrant juice," said Little Red Riding Hood. "Grandmother is ill and Mother has sent these to help her to get well again."

"Where does your grandmother live, Little Red Riding Hood?" continued the wolf.

"Just a little further into the forest," answered Little Red Riding Hood. "Her cottage stands under three large oak trees."

"What a tender young creature this is!" thought the wolf. "She will make a more juicy mouthful than the old woman! But, if I am cunning, I should manage to eat both!"

So the wolf strolled along beside Little Red Riding Hood for a little while.

"Look at all the pretty flowers under the trees," he said. "Are they not beautiful? And can you hear the birds singing? You should stop and enjoy these pleasures instead of walking straight along the path."

Then the wolf said goodbye to Little Red Riding Hood and set off quickly for Grandmother's cottage.

Little Red Riding Hood did as the wolf suggested and looked around her. The forest was indeed a lovely place. The sunbeams danced through the trees, the ground was carpeted with beautiful flowers and overhead the birds sang merrily.

"I shall pick a bunch of fresh flowers for my grandmother," thought Little Red Riding Hood. "They will cheer her up."

So she wandered further and further from the path, gathering the prettiest of the flowers.

By now the wolf had reached Grandmother's cottage. He knocked at the door.

"Who is there?" called Grandmother.

"Little Red Riding Hood," replied the wolf in a high voice. "I have brought you a cake and some blackcurrant juice."

"Press the latch, open the door and walk in, my dear," said Grandmother. "I am so weak that I cannot get up."

The wolf pressed the latch, opened the door and walked in.

Without saying a word, the wolf went straight to the bed and gobbled Grandmother up in one mouthful.

Then he put on one of her nightdresses and a nightcap which he pulled well down over his eyes. He drew the curtains and got into bed, pulling the bedclothes well up to his chin.

Then he waited.

Meanwhile Little Red Riding Hood had wandered far from the path, for the loveliest flowers always seemed to be furthest away.

When she had gathered a pretty posy of flowers, she returned to the path and went on her way.

When Little Red Riding Hood arrived at her grandmother's cottage, she was surprised to find the door standing wide open.

"Good morning, Grandmother!" called out Little Red Riding Hood as she went inside, but she got no reply.

Then Little Red Riding Hood began to feel rather uneasy. She went up to the bed and drew back the curtains.

There lay her grandmother, with her cap pulled down to her eyes and the bedclothes pulled up to her chin, looking very strange.

"Oh, Grandmother!" cried Little Red Riding Hood. "What big ears you have!"

"All the better to hear you with, my dear," came the reply.

"Oh, Grandmother! What big eyes you have!"

"All the better to see you with, my dear!"

"Oh, Grandmother! What big hands you have!"

"All the better to hug you with, my dear!"

"Oh, Grandmother! What big teeth you have!"

"All the better to eat you with!"

With these words, the wolf jumped out of bed and gobbled up Little Red Riding Hood in one mouthful.

Then he climbed into bed, lay down and fell fast asleep.

Soon he began to snore. He snored so loudly that the cottage shook.

Just at that time, Little Red Riding Hood's father was passing near by. He heard the awful snores coming from the cottage and thought he had better go in to see why Little Red Riding Hood's grandmother was snoring so loudly.

When he went up to the bed, he saw the wolf lying there.

"You wicked creature!" he cried in a rage.

With one blow of his axe he killed the wolf, and pulled him out of the bed. Then he had an idea! Perhaps the wolf had swallowed Grandmother whole and perhaps he was in time to save her.

Little Red Riding Hood's father cut open the wolf, hoping to find Grandmother inside, alive.

Imagine his surprise when up popped a little red hood and out jumped Little Red Riding Hood!

"Oh! How frightened I was!" cried Little Red Riding Hood. "It was as dark as night inside the wolf!"

Then her father helped Grandmother out. She was still alive but was feeling very unwell.

Little Red Riding Hood and her father put Grandmother into bed. They gave her some of the cake and some blackcurrant juice. Soon she was sitting up and feeling much better.

They were happy and relieved all to be alive and well.

Little Red Riding Hood's father took her by the hand and led her back home. When Little Red Riding Hood's mother heard their story she was shocked, and she gave her little girl a big hug.

Little Red Riding Hood promised that she would never wander off the path through the forest again. And she never, ever did.

A History of
Little Red Riding Hood

The story of *Little Red Riding Hood* has inspired picture books, films and pantomimes. However, the story probably started life as a folk tale in France or Italy. It was first written down and published by French writer Charles Perrault in 1697.

Perrault is remembered for writing the early versions of many of the fairy tales that are still popular today, including *Cinderella*, *Puss in Boots* and *Sleeping Beauty*, in his *Histoires ou Contes du Temps Passé (Stories or Tales of Past Times)*.

In 1812, the Brothers Grimm published a new version of *Little Red*

Riding Hood, called 'Rotkappen' in German, which means 'Little Red Cap' in English.

Over the years, the story's popularity has remained. The Ladybird version, written by Vera Southgate, is the one best-known by many people today.

Collect more fantastic
LADYBIRD 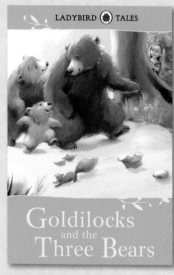 TALES

Cinderella

9781409311072

Goldilocks
and the
Three Bears

9781409311119

Jack
and the
Beanstalk

9781409311102

Little Red
Riding Hood

9781409311126

The Gingerbread Man

9781409311096

The Three Little Pigs

9781409311089

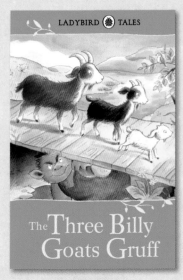

The Three Billy Goats Gruff

9781409311065

Hansel and Gretel

9781409311133

Endpapers taken from series 606d,
first published in 1964

A catalogue record for this book is available from the British Library

Published by Ladybird Books Ltd
80 Strand London WC2R 0RL
A Penguin Company

007

ISBN: 978-1-40931-112-6

Printed in China